ADH-Me!

By Dr. John S. Hutton
Illustrated by Lisa M. Griffin

blue manatee press
Cincinnati, OH

www.bluemanateepress.com

Published by blue manatee press,
Cincinnati, Ohio.
blue manatee press and associated logo
are registered trademarks of Arete Ventures, LLC.

First Edition: Fall, 2016.

Library of Congress Cataloging-In-Publication Data
ADH-Me! / by John S. Hutton; illustrated by Lisa Griffin—1st ed.
Summary: Written by a pediatrician and health literacy expert,
ADH-Me! is an empowering journey from the perspective of a child learning to
live and succeed with ADHD. An accessible, rhyming narrative and inviting
illustrations help families know what to expect from diagnosis through stages
of treatment, reminding readers that love and support are the surest means to
a happy ending.

Hardcover Edition: ISBN-13: 978-1-936669-51-6
Paperback Edition: ISBN-13: 978-1-936669-52-3

[Juvenile Fiction – Health & Daily Living / General. 2. Juvenile Fiction – Social Themes
/ Self-Esteem & Self-Reliance.]
Printed in the USA.

Artwork was created using graphite for the original line art, then colored and
composed using Corel Painter.
Editorial design by Mayte Suarez

To my parents - for always believing in me.

- John

For Alyssa, Ryan and Jack...
who have inspired me from the very beginning.

- Lisa

As far back as I can recall
(starting when I was very small)

I've daydreamed, gazing into space,
climbed and jumped all over the place.

The older I got,
the more trouble came.
Kids could be mean.
Some called me names.

My parents got mad,
teachers did, too.
Wherever I went,
I didn't know what to do.

So many troubles
made me feel sad.
Sad turned to angry,
my behavior turned bad:

talking back,

acting out,

fighting,

class clown.

Nothing helped.
I felt worse,
down, down, down...

"Try harder," they'd say,
"Focus! Pay attention!"
"Don't you remember the
things that I mention?"

I didn't. I'd try,
but they'd just slip away,
like Remember Fish darting
through my brain each day.

"We have to do something," my parents finally said.
We went to the doctor with feelings of dread.

I squirmed as they talked for a really long time,
then told me I had a...*thing,* but would be fine.

"Attention Deficit Hyperactivity Disorder."

(I wish they'd invented a name that was shorter.)

- **Attention** means focus, to see and to hear.
- **Deficit** means not quite enough (oh dear).
- **Hyperactivity**, too much jumping around.
- **Disorder**, unhealthy, but help can be found.

Where did it come from?
Was it contagious?

Was it like poison ivy?
Did it have stages?

"No," they said,
"ADHD's nothing like that.
It's caused by a difference
in how brain cells chat."

I felt weird at first,
then learned that I'm not.
ADHD's a thing
lots of people have got.

I was born with it,
which makes sense because
Dad thinks he has it,
Uncle Drew *definitely* does.

Artists, scientists,
business owners too,
full of energy and ideas
to create something new.

Also bravery, fun, and kindness of heart.
Best of all: kids with ADHD are smart!

Together, we made a plan to test
some changes to help me be my best.

We'd come back in a month and see how it went.
"I want to get better," is the wish that I sent.

Changes at home
started when we got back.
A "to-do" list on the wall
helped me keep track.

It felt good getting work done
and helping with chores,
eating healthy, early bedtime
(I even tried not to snore).

Believe

TO-DO LIST

o Make sure all homework and school
    supplies are in my backpack

o Put laundry in the hamper

o Clear dishes and sweep kitchen floor

o Bring cleats for soccer practice

This was hard,
but I could watch
up to 2 hours a day,
after homework, 'to-dos,'
and fun, healthy play.

A month later, my doctor said,
"Better," then sighed:
"The scores on these
reports are still too high."

"Still squirmy,
forgetting at home and at school,
still getting in trouble,
frustrated by rules."

And so, a new office,
a nice lady named Sue.
We talked about feelings
and things I can do:

Slow down. Breathe...
Think smart, strong and tall!
Work with my parents
on the list on my wall.

At school,
there were
big changes, too.
We had meetings
with teachers
and Mr. Lou.

$20 + (8+4) \div 3$

$3 \times (4+2) \div 2$

$60 + (18+7)$

$24 \div 6 + 3 \times (6-4)$

IEP

They gave me some tests
to see what I need:
extra help and work time
at just the right speed.

Checking back
with my doctor
the following season,

my feelings
were better,
focus wasn't
for some reason.

"Medicine is the next step,"
my doctor said.
My parents said nervously,
"Let's go ahead."

Each morning,
I had a pill to take,
then breakfast and a
Daily Plan to make.

The medicine could make
my appetite slack,
so I made sure to eat lunch
and a healthy snack.

We went back to my doctor
to make sure all was well.
There were so many
exciting things to tell!

We agreed it was great,
but if anything changed,
a new plan for me
would be arranged.

My teachers and friends
soon noticed too:

"Good job!"

"Sit here!"

"Can we play with you?"

Through "to-do" lists,
sharing feelings,
and just being a kid,
I got better and better–
look what I did!

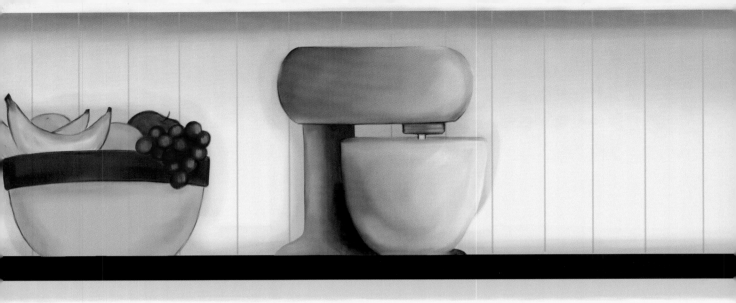

It's amazing! I was squirmy, in trouble and mad.
We made changes and each day I felt more glad.

Every person is different, it's clear to see,
but I'm oh-so-proud to be A-D-H-Me!

ADH-Me! Facts and Helpful Tips:

- Attention Deficit Hyperactivity Disorder (ADHD) is a **clinical** diagnosis, which means there's no blood test or x-ray that can tell if someone has it. It's made by talks between parents, teachers, doctors, and the child.

- ADHD is 75% **heritable**, which means if a child has it, there's a good chance a close relative does too.

- ADHD is usually diagnosed around **kindergarten** (when kids have to sit longer for lessons) and almost always before age 12.

- ADHD diagnosis involves **inattentive** (daydreamy) and **hyperactive** (squirmy) symptoms. Lots of kids (and grownups) have these, but for ADHD, these symptoms need to cause problems in school and at home for at least **6 months.**

- Kids with ADHD often struggle with **reading** (holding words in mind), and do better with extra help at school.

- ADHD is very **treatable**. Many people with ADHD, including doctors, lawyers, teachers, athletes, and artists, achieve amazing things.

- **Treatment** of ADHD starts with making changes at home and school, then working with a counselor and/or medicine as needed.

- **Medicine** can be very helpful, but it's important to watch for side effects including problems with sleep, appetite, and mood. A doctor will help look out for these.

- **These things help ADHD get better:**
  - Getting a good night's sleep (9 hours or more)
  - Eating a healthy diet with lots of water and not too much sugar
  - Getting plenty of exercise, including playing outside
  - Reducing screen time (TV, video games, Internet, apps) to less than 2 hours a day and none in the bedroom
  - Making checklists of things to do: chores, homework, activities, etc.

- No matter what, keep a positive attitude, do your best, and be **proud** of who you are!

Reference: http://www.cdc.gov/ncbddd/adhd

My To-Do List

1. _____

2. _____

3. _____

4. _____

5. _____

6. _____

7. _____

8. _____

9. _____

10. _____

```
+
E HUTTO

Hutton, John
ADH-me! /
Central PICTURE-BK
10/16
```